Sweet Dreams, Supergirl is published by
Capstone Young Readers
a Capstone imprint
1710 Roe Crest Drive
North Mankato, Minnesota 56003
www.mycapstone.com

STAR39805

Cataloging-in-Publication Data is available on the
Library of Congress website.

ISBN: 978-1-62370-998-3 (jacketed hardcover)

Jacket and book design by Bob Lentz

Printed in China.
010730S18

words by **MICHAEL DAHL**

pictures by **OMAR LOZANO**

Sweet Dreams, SUPERGIRL™

Supergirl based on characters created by
JERRY SIEGEL and **JOE SHUSTER**
by special arrangement with the Jerry Siegel family

CAPSTONE YOUNG READERS
a Capstone imprint

. . . until moonlit night . . .

A hero bursts with POW!-WHAM!-BOOM! energy . . .

. . . and each night, she'll have a story to share.

Each day, a hero welcomes helping hands . . .

All day, a super hero travels far and wide . . .

. . . so at night, she snuggles up, safe and warm.

All day, a hero faces many challenges alone.

But at night,
others are
always there
for her.

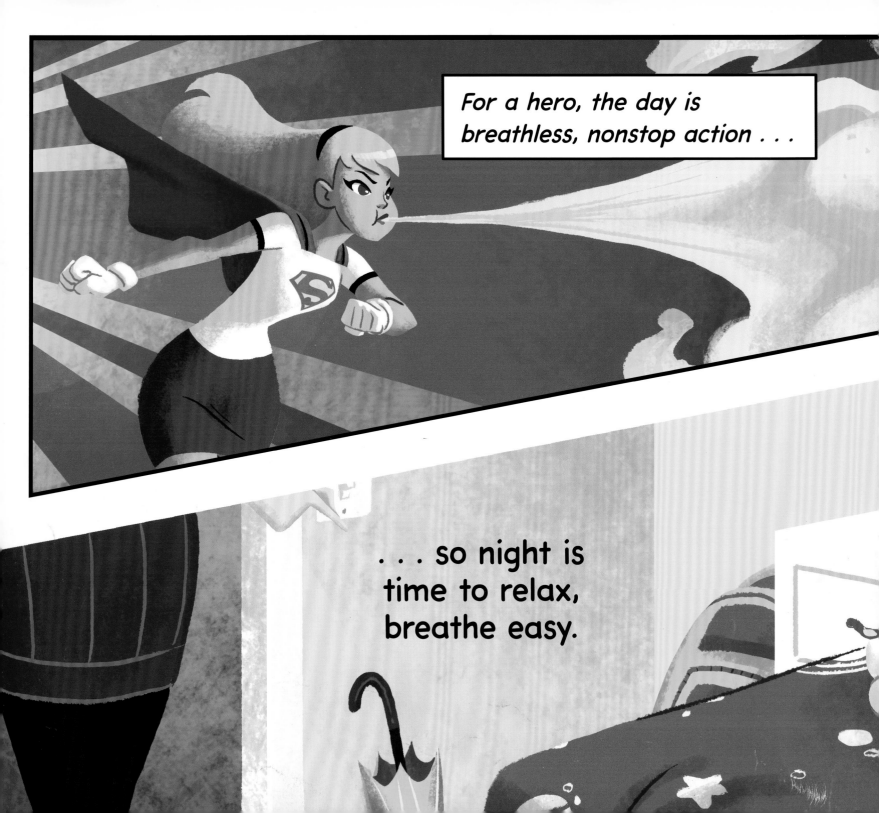

A super hero bravely faces each and every day.

And each and
every night,
she must be
courageous too.

For after a day with eyes wide open . . .

. . . the time has come to rest them.

Tomorrow, once again . . .

. . . the world needs a hero . . .

. . . to soar . . .

Sweet dreams, Supergirl.

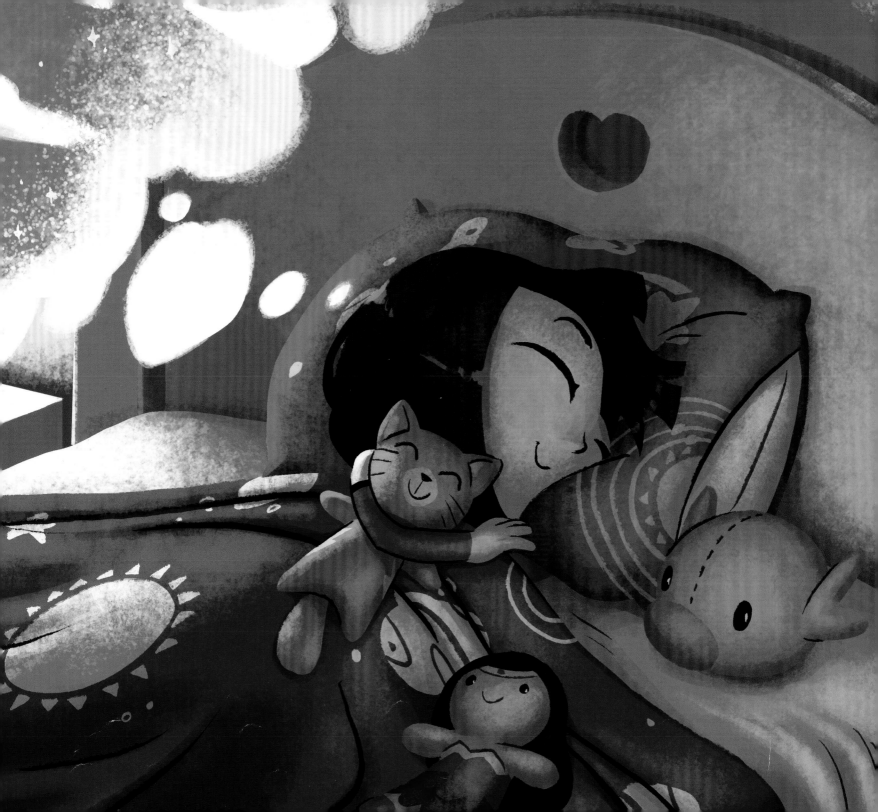

Sweet Dreams CHECKLIST!

Share Stories

Say Goodnight

Snuggle Up

Breathe Easy

Stay Brave

Dream Big